© 1996 Disney Enterprises, Inc.
Published by Hachette Partworks Ltd
ISBN: 978-1-906965-01-3
Date of Printing: November 2009
Printed in Singapore by Tien Wah Press

Early one spring
morning the quiet of
the woods was broken
by a *thump-thump-
thumping* sound.

It was Thumper the rabbit, loudly thumping his foot on a log.

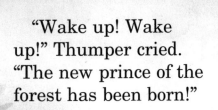

"Wake up! Wake up!" Thumper cried. "The new prince of the forest has been born!"

The animals all followed Thumper to a thicket,
where a doe nestled with her sleeping fawn.

"Congratulations!" Owl said to the mother deer.
"This is a very special day!"

The mother deer gently nudged the fawn.
"Wake up," she said. "Meet your new friends!"
The fawn tried to stand on his new legs.

"Look, he's getting up!" Thumper cried,
hopping over to watch. "Kind of wobbly, isn't he?"
he remarked.

Before long the fawn was up on all four legs.
He peeked through his legs to look at Thumper.

"What are you going to call him?"
Thumper asked.

"I'll call him Bambi," the doe said.
Bambi seemed to like his name.

Bambi and Thumper soon became best friends.
Every day Thumper taught Bambi something new
about the forest.

"Those are birds," Thumper told Bambi one day.
"Say *bird*."

"Burr-burr-BIRD!" Bambi shouted, frightening away the little forest creatures.

"You did it!" Thumper laughed. "You can talk!" Bambi was very proud of himself. He wanted to try again.

"That's a butterfly!"
Thumper explained.

"And those pretty
things are flowers."

Just then a little black-and-white face
poked out of the flower patch. "Flower," Bambi
said.

Thumper giggled. "That's not a flower!"

"He can call me Flower if he wants to," said
the skunk. "I don't mind."

Spring turned into summer. One warm day
Bambi's mother said, "Follow me. We are going to
the meadow."

"What's the meadow?" Bambi asked.

His mother said, "It has grass and room to
run, and you can play with some of the other
deer there."

"Thumper told me there were other deer in the
forest, but I haven't seen any," Bambi said.
He couldn't wait to meet them!

At the edge of the woods Bambi could see an open space with waving grass. He was about to run out when his mother stopped him.

"Bambi, wait! You must always be sure that the meadow is safe before you run out," she told him. "The meadow is wide and open, so we have to be very careful."

Bambi's mother made sure that the meadow was safe. Then she called Bambi out of hiding.

What fun Bambi had
at the meadow! He and
Thumper chased a frog to a
pond. The frog croaked and
jumped into the water.

Bambi bent down
to have a drink of the
cool water. He saw
another little fawn's
face join his in the
reflection. *Who is this?*
he wondered.

Bambi ran to find his mother.

"This is Faline," his mother told him.

"Do you want to play?" Faline asked Bambi.
He nodded. So the two fawns began chasing each
other around the meadow. Bambi and Faline quickly
became friends.

Suddenly all became
still on the meadow.
Bambi and Faline looked
up. A strong deer with
large antlers was walking
slowly toward them. The
young prince stared back
at the great buck.

The buck turned his head and looked at Bambi kindly. Then he continued on his way back into the woods. Bambi and his mother watched him go.

"Who is he?" Bambi whispered to his mother. "He is your father," Bambi's mother answered, "the Great Prince of the Forest."

Summer turned into autumn. The days grew
shorter, and soon golden leaves began to fall from
the trees. The wind swept across the meadow, and
the icy water of the stream made Bambi shiver.
Winter was coming.

Bambi woke up one morning to see the forest had turned white.

"What's all this white stuff?" he asked.

"It's snow," his mother explained.

"Winter has come."

Bambi stepped out of his den. PLOP! A big pile of snow landed right on his head!

"C'mon!" called Thumper. "Let's go sliding on the stiff water."

The two friends hurried to the pond.

"*Wheeee!*" Thumper laughed as he slid across the ice.

Bambi ran to follow him. CRASH! Down he fell on the slippery ice.

"You have to keep both ends up at the same time," Thumper explained, trying to help.

Thumper gave Bambi a push, and the little deer slipped and slid across the pond until he landed right outside Flower's den.

Bambi and Thumper wanted the little skunk to play with them.

"No, thanks. I'll see you in the spring," Flower said with a yawn. He always slept right through the winter!

The snow had covered the plants on the
ground, and Bambi and the other deer had a
hard time finding food. The little fawn didn't
like eating the chewy bark from the trees, but
there was nothing else to eat.

"Winter sure is long," Bambi sighed.
He missed the soft, green grass!

"I think there might be some grass at the meadow," Bambi's mother said. "Let's go and see."

Bambi was nibbling some tender grass when his mother raised her head. She sensed there was danger nearby.

Suddenly his mother cried,
"Run, Bambi, run!"

The little fawn heard a
thunderous noise as he dashed
through the woods to safety. He
reached the thicket, but his mother
wasn't behind him any longer.
"Mother!" he called.

Then Bambi's father
came out of the forest.
"Your mother can't be
with you any longer.
Now you must be brave.
Come, my son," the
Great Prince said.
So Bambi followed him
into the snowy woods.

At last the sun warmed the earth, the flowers
bloomed, and the tiny birds began to sing happy
songs once more.

"Oh, my," yawned Owl. "It seems that spring is
here again!"

Bambi and his new
friends had grown up
over the winter.

"I suppose you'll all
be twitterpated now that spring
is here!" Owl told them.
"What does that mean?" they
asked. "You'll fall in love"
Owl said. "Just wait and see."

Owl was right. Flower met a pretty girl skunk...

... Thumper flirted with a sweet girl rabbit...

... and when Faline saw Bambi, she gave him a big kiss. They were all twitterpated!

Bambi and Faline still liked to go to the meadow together, but instead of playing tag, they quietly walked side by side.

One morning Bambi woke up to strange
smell in the wind. He left Faline and climbed
a mountain, where he was met by his father.
The two deer saw a stream of smoke rising
from the woods below. Fire!

Faline woke up and began to search for Bambi. The smell of smoke was stronger now. Suddenly a group of dogs began to chase her!

Faline was trapped by
the growling pack of dogs.
But then Bambi raced to
her rescue!

Bambi lowered his head
and drove the dogs away
with his pointed antlers.
"Run Faline!" he shouted. The
young doe jumped across the
cliffs to safety.

Bambi leaped across the cliffs to follow Faline.

He reached the
other side, but
the young prince
was hurt.

A thick cloud
of smoke moved
closer and closer.

Bambi heard a familiar voice.
"Get up, Bambi! The fire is almost here!"
It was the Great Prince of the Forest.
Bambi struggled to his feet.

The two deer raced through
the forest to escape the terrible
fire. Bambi and his father
came to the river. Bambi closed
his eyes and jumped, soaring
over the waterfall.
They were safe!

All the forest creatures had gathered on an
island in the middle of the river. Faline rushed
over to Bambi.

They sadly watched as the forest burned.
But the fire did not destroy the forest completely.

By the next spring the trees were green again.
Thump-thump-thump! Thumper was calling the animals of the forest. "Come and see!" he shouted.

Thumper and Flower and their children hurried over to see Faline. By her side, blinking in the sunlight, were two tiny fawns.

"Prince Bambi must be very proud," said Owl.
Owl was right once again. For Bambi stood proudly watching over his family as the new Great Prince of the Forest!